D1572094

Piercing The Veil

Bill Myers

Jeff Gerke, Angela Hunt, and Alton Gansky

BILL MYERS

Published by Amaris Media International.
Copyright © 2016 Bill Myers
Cover Design: Angela Hunt
Photo credits: ©Michael Pettigrew and ©xixinxing

ISBN-13: 978-0692697634
ISBN-10: 0692697632

For more information, visit us on Facebook:
https://www.facebook.com/pages/Harbingers/705107309586877

or *www.harbingersseries.com*.

HARBINGERS

A novella series by
Bill Myers, Frank Peretti, Angela Hunt,
and Alton Gansky

In this fast-paced world with all its demands, the four of us wanted to try something new. Instead of the longer novel format, we wanted to write something equally as engaging but that could be read in one or two sittings—on the plane, waiting to pick up the kids from soccer, or as an evening's read.

We also wanted to play. As friends and seasoned novelists, we thought it would be fun to create a game we could participate in together. The rules were simple:

Rule #1

Each of us will write as if we were one of the characters in the series:

Bill Myers will write as Brenda, the street-hustling tattoo artist who sees images of the future.

Frank Peretti will write as the professor, the atheist ex-priest ruled by logic.

Angela Hunt will write as Andi, the professor's brilliant-but-geeky assistant who sees inexplicable patterns.

Alton Gansky will write as Tank, the naïve, big-hearted jock with a surprising connection to a healing power.

Rule #2

Instead of the four of us writing one novella together (we're friends but not crazy), we would write it like a TV series. There would be an overarching storyline into which we'd plug our individual novellas, with each story written from our character's point of view.

If you're keeping track, this is the order:

Harbingers #1—*The Call*—Bill Myers
Harbingers #2—*The Haunted*—Frank Peretti
Harbingers #3—*The Sentinels*—Angela Hunt
Harbingers #4—*The Girl*—Alton Gansky

Volumes #1-4 omnibus: *Cycle One: Invitation*

Harbingers #5—*The Revealing*—Bill Myers
Harbingers #6—*Infestation*—Frank Peretti
Harbingers #7—*Infiltration*—Angela Hunt
Harbingers #8—*The Fog*—Alton Gansky

Volumes #5-8 omnibus: *Cycle Two: Mosaic*

Harbingers #9—*Leviathan*—Bill Myers
Harbingers #10—*The Mind Pirates*—Frank Peretti
Harbingers #11—*Hybrids*—Angela Hunt
Harbingers #12—*The Village*—Alton Gansky

Volumes 9-12 omnibus: *Cycle Three: The Probing*

There you have it, at least for now. We hope you'll find these as entertaining in the reading as we are in the writing.

Bill, Frank, Angie, Al

Chapter 1

I hate Vegas.

Sorry if that messes with your white, middle class dreams for a vacation. Sorrier still if you're some city councilman that wants to sue my butt for talking trash. (Good luck with that—you can have the trailer—my shop, too, the way all this traveling messes with my business).

Anyway, that's why I didn't take Daniel, why I swung over and dropped him off at my mom's in Arizona before driving over here. I don't care how much he begs, Vegas ain't no place for a kid, 'specially one with his unique sensitivities. I know I said that before, 'specially during our little visit to North Carolina. But there's way too much trash goin' on here that folks don't see (or don't want to). Lucky for me, I was one of the smart ones. Got out before too much damage was done. But there's plenty of other sisters, brothers too, who weren't so lucky.

I'd been on the 93 almost three hours now—the afternoon sun hitting my eyes, and the oven-hot wind roaring through the open windows of my beater Toyota. Not to cool things down, but to dry up sweat so I ain't swimming in it.

Last week I got another one of those texts from "Unknown Caller." It was tellin' me to pick up Andi and Tank, aka Cowboy, at the airport, 3:15 today. It's almost 5:00, courtesy of my overheating radiator. But they know I'll be there. We're always there for each other. Like a bad habit.

Still, these little outings, they're taking their toll. You'd think it would be easier without the professor and his attitude. But no. Not by a long shot. Truth is, I miss him almost as much as Andi does. We were entirely different, fought like cats and dogs, but somehow he got me. And I got him. And now . . . I don't know.

I arrived at the airport and pulled into Terminal One. Sure enough, there was Andi in her flaming red hair. She was melting in the heat and having her ears talked off by Cowboy.

I gave a honk and pulled up.

"There she is!" Cowboy grabbed his duffle bag and, despite Andi's protests, her backpack, too. "Boy, it's good to see you," he said as he opened the door and tossed their stuff in the back.

"It sure is," Andi said.

I could tell by the look of relief she wasn't lying. Cowboy's a great guy, all 6' 4", 275 pounds of him. But he likes to talk. 'Specially when it's to someone he's trying to impress. Course she's told him a dozen times she's not interested, but the loveable lug is as persistent as he is loyal.

He opened the front door, motioning for Andi to take the seat. "Whew," he laughed. "It's so hot here I bet hens are laying hard-boiled eggs."

Andi cut me a look of desperation. She's a sweet kid and doesn't know how to be rude. Come to think of it, Cowboy's the same. But that's where the similarities stop.

As Cowboy shut her door and headed for the back, I asked him, "Sure you don't want the front seat?"

"Thanks, but I'm good," he said. Course he wasn't. You could tell by the way he gasped and grunted, trying to pull in his legs.

"Where's Daniel?" Andi asked as she looked for the seat belt.

"Don't bother," I said. "It hasn't worked for years."

"And Daniel?"

"Not this time."

She gave me a look. "Are you seeing something dangerous?"

"No more than usual. But me and Vegas, we got a history he don't need to be exposed to."

After the usual grinding of gears, I found first and we pulled out.

Cowboy leaned forward to join us. "But you are seeing stuff, right?"

I nodded to the sketchpad on the dashboard.

Andi grabbed it and started flipping pages. There was plenty of drawings from our past encounters— that empty chair in the Vatican, Littlefoot from whatever reality she was in, even the sketch of ourselves (which was also tatted on Cowboy's arm). But it wasn't until she came to the picture of the flying dragon that she came to a stop. It was pretty detailed—red and purple with shiny scales, and little arms and hands under its wings.

"This?" she asked.

"For starters."

She flipped through the other sketches I'd been seeing in my head the past week or so . . . like the green recliner with all sorts of electrical junk around it, or the snowflakes, lots and lots of snowflakes, or the creepy, frog-faced gargoyles. Lots of them, too.

"I sure don't like them things," Cowboy said, referring to the gargoyles.

"Why not?" Andi asked.

"I don't want to get weird on you . . ."

"No, go ahead."

"It's just . . . that's how some folks describe demons."

Andi took a breath and closed the pad. "Well, it looks like we might be in for a wild ride this time."

I flipped the dreads out of my face. "So what else is new?"

She nodded and we all got kind of quiet. 'Cause there's one thing you can say about my sketches: They're never wrong.

Chapter 2

No problem finding our hotel. Besides the name, Preston Towers, there were two twelve-foot high, hitching posts out front. The internet said it was one of the city's finest, right on the Strip. No surprise there. Our employers, they may be all secretive and stuff, never letting us know who they are . . . but they sure know how to treat us.

The car jockeys, faces leathery from the sun, were all over us—opening doors, grabbing luggage, anything for a tip.

"Nah, fellas, we're good," Cowboy said. "We got it." But they were pretty pushy so our good ol' boy let 'em have their way.

Not me. When they asked for the keys I said I'd park it.

"Actually," a tall brother said. "I'm afraid that's not possible."

"Actually, I'll make it possible."

"We're the only ones with access to the garage."

"Then I'll park outside the garage."

"There's nothing close. The nearest—"

"We good?" I called to Cowboy as he finished loading up the cart.

He nodded.

"Ma'am, if you'll just give me the keys."

"I said *I'll* park it."

"The nearest spot is four blocks away and even at that—"

"I can use the exercise."

I wasn't being a jerk. As a single mom with Daniel and all, I got no need to line someone else's pocket. So after some gear grinding, I pulled onto the Strip leaving behind my customary cloud of blue smoke.

I eventually took a left on Stan Mallin Drive. I'd gone a couple more blocks when this kid, I don't know where he came from, is suddenly in front of me. I slammed on my brakes, but my bumper caught him and, 'fore I knew it, he's sailing onto my hood, then rolling off and onto the road.

I leaped out and ran toward him. "You all right? You okay?"

He lay there, not moving. I dropped to my knees, swearing and praying at the same time, when he suddenly jumps up, pushes me out of the way and runs for my car.

"Hey!" I scrambled to my feet. "Hey!" I took off after him. He was already inside, slamming the door, but no way was I going to let him jack my car. Once I got there, I reached through the window and grabbed his shirt. He tried pushing me away, at the same time fighting with the gearshift. But neither of us was goin' anywhere.

I leaned back and punched him in the face. Not hard, but when you aim for the nose it don't take much. He yelped in surprise and I hit him again. This time there was blood. A real gusher. He swore, hands shooting to his face, which gave me plenty of time to grab the door and throw it open.

"What are you doing?" he yelled.

"What am *I* doing?"

"I don't have time for this!"

I tried dragging him out but he wasn't so cooperative, so I began rabbit-punching him. He got the message.

"All right!" he cried, "All right!"

"This is my car!" I threw in some R-rated language. "Mine!"

"I get it, I get it!" He held up hands, protecting his face like a little girl. "You made your point!"

I paused as he climbed out of the car, then hit him one more time just 'cause he pissed me off.

"Alright!"

He was a good-looking kid, early twenties and from what I could tell, pretty ripped. Even with his hands over his face there was no doubt he was a babe magnet. But it wasn't his looks that got me. It was the dragon tattoo on his right arm. Exactly like the one I'd sketched. Down to the little hands under its wings.

"Who are you?" I yelled.

He spotted something behind me. "It doesn't matter."

"What?"

He motioned down the street. "They're the ones to worry about."

I turned and saw two casino thugs in suits racing towards us. "What do they want?"

"Me," he said. "And now you."

They were big guys and no doubt carrying. And by the look on their faces, they weren't from any hospitality center.

"You running from them?" I asked.

He didn't answer. I turned back to look at him. Actually his tattoo. Then I turned to the thugs. They were thirty feet away.

"All right, get in!" I ordered.

He didn't need a second invite. As he ran to the passenger side, I slid behind the wheel. I didn't know who he was or what they wanted, but I did know that tattoo. And, like I said, the boys didn't look like they wanted to chit-chat. I found first, stepped on the gas, and left behind my trademark cloud of choking blue smoke.

Chapter 3

"Nice friends you got," I said.

He checked his nose for the third or fourth time. "You're not exactly Miss Congeniality."

I motioned to the blood on his hands. "Don't get any of that on my seat."

"I think you broke it."

"Next time try askin' politely. There's napkins in the glove compartment."

He tried opening it. I reached over and slammed it with my fist a couple times before it popped open.

"What they got against you, anyways?" I asked.

He grabbed a couple of the napkins, courtesy of Burger King, and dabbed at the blood. "I come into town every few weeks, do some playing and pick up some cash."

"You that good?"

"I'm better than good, lady."

"You a card counter?"

"Please, even with your limited skills you should know better than that."

I didn't know what he was talking about but I was disliking him already. And since I'd done my community service for the night, I began to pull over.

"What are you doing?"

"Dropping you off."

"Uh, I don't think so. Not me." The kid was as arrogant as he was good looking. "I live over forty miles from here."

"Nice night for a walk," I said.

"But . . . you will take me home."

"In your dreams."

"Actually, it would be in *your* dreams."

I shot him a withering look.

He shrugged. "But don't take it personally. I'm not into older chicks."

I brought the car to a stop, reached past him and opened the door. "Goodnight."

"But . . . you saw the tattoo, right? The dragon? The one you've been drawing for the last two weeks?"

"How did—"

He grinned. "And that image will haunt you, unless you drive me back to my lab."

"Your lab?"

"You didn't see that? You didn't draw it? Man you *are* an amateur." He sighed. "Another reason I'm not interested in joining your team."

"My . . .?"

"Come on, I'm not an idiot, Belinda."

"Belinda?"

"Your name."

"Try Brenda."

"Close enough."

"*Who* are you?"

He gave another sigh. "My name is Chad Thorton. And you and your little band of wannabe warriors have come to recruit me."

"Recruit you?"

"To replace that old fart who disappeared."

He definitely had my attention. "Are you talking about—"

"And I'll tell you just like I told your handlers, I'm not interested in working with rookies." Before I could respond, he explained, "The football jock, the red-headed babe, and your kid—though he's probably got more potential than the rest of you combined—at least that's what you think."

"What do you know what I think?"

"Come on, lady. That's what I do." He tapped his temple. "That's *my* specialty." He glanced out the back window. "Now can we please get going?"

I stared at him.

He turned and grinned.

I swore, found first, and pulled back into traffic.

He settled back into the seat.

I found Chad Thorton to be almost as informative as he was obnoxious. Almost. As his own biggest fan, he spent the entire drive talking about himself . . .

His childhood:

"As far back as I can remember, people, *real important* people have wanted to study and capitalize on my extraordinary abilities."

I cut him another look.

He gave me another shrug. "What can I say, it's a gift. Similar to yours, but obviously far more developed. No offense."

Offense was taken.

After that, he started going on about our organization:

"Oh, yeah, you guys have been trying to recruit me for months. You know, to help you fight the, what do you call it . . . the Gate?"

I gripped the wheel a little tighter.

He saw it and laughed. "Sure, I know about the Gate. Not everything, just what I've read off your handlers. The Gate, they're some uber-secret organization working side by side with extra-dimensionals to take over the world." He chuckled. "And your little group is supposed to help stop them."

I caught my breath, then tried to sound cool and unimpressed. "And that doesn't interest you, stopping them?"

"Nope."

"That's it? *Nope*?"

"That's right."

"And these other people," I said, "what did you call them—our *handlers*?"

"Yeah, the Watchers."

For the second time I caught my breath. Did he actually know their name?

He continued. "Good guys, I suppose. But the odds are definitely not in their favor."

"You called them the Watchers."

He turned to me and cocked his head "Don't tell me you didn't know their name?"

I said nothing.

He broke out laughing. "Priceless, man. You're working for an organization and you don't even know who they are."

"I didn't say that."

"You didn't have to." He flashed me that grin and tapped his temple.

I felt my ears growing hot. I looked back to the road.

He continued. "One thing you can say about them though, they sure got the bucks. And not just for your plane tickets and hotels. These dudes, they got more money than you and I can imagine."

"Why do you say that?"

"How else would you explain San Diego? All those deaths, that building destroyed. And not a word of it in the press? Talk about hush money, or—" he shrugged again— "maybe they got their own mind games."

"You know about San Diego?"

"Only what I've read off the first recruiter. Or the second. I forget."

"You've met them? Personally?"

"The Watchers? Of course. Well, their representatives." He looked back at me. "You haven't?"

Before I could answer he shook his head and chuckled again. "Well I guess that lets you know how important I am, at least compared to you guys."

I glanced at his nose, wondering if it needed more adjusting. Lucky for him, I was able to contain myself. I hoped he appreciated the effort.

Chapter 4

I'd barely entered the "lab" with the kid before a pretty, twenty-something in wire-rimmed glasses and a white stocking cap ran toward him. "Your nose!"

"It's nothing."

"But . . . it's broken," she said. "How—?"

"It's not broken," he said scornfully. "Don't you think I'd know if it's broken?"

Her eyes shot to me, then back to him. "How did it happen?"

"Long story. Grab us some coffee, will you?"

"But—"

He brushed past her. "Coffee."

She hesitated.

"Now."

"Sure thing." She turned to leave.

"Belinda takes hers black, no cream or sugar." He threw me a look and grinned. "Right?"

I didn't bother to answer.

The building was on Highway 15, north of Vegas, the middle of nowhere. Except for the occasional semi there were no other lights or signs of civilization. It wasn't much to look at, more like a giant shed, one of those old Quonset huts the military used to use.

But inside, things were a little different.

"I've only got a couple minutes to spare," he said, "but I can show you around." Without waiting for an answer, he started the tour.

"The place was used by the Army from the mid-seventies until about 1990. It was called the Dragon Stealth Program." He gestured to a painting over the entrance we'd just walked through. "Look familiar?"

I could only stare. The image was identical to the one I'd been sketching . . . and to the one tatted on his arm.

"The boys and girls at Stanford Research Institute teamed up with Army Intelligence to experiment with remote viewing."

"Remote viewing?"

"You know. Where you send your spirit out of your body to travel and spy on enemy instalations."

I frowned.

"You never heard of it?"

"Yeah, well . . . in a way."

He snickered. "Liar."

Course he was right, but I wasn't going to let him know. Not with his attitude.

"You guys really are amateurs, aren't you?"

I didn't think it possible, but I was liking him

even less. We walked across the worn linoleum floor to a heavy padded door, like they have in recording studios. He pulled it open and we stepped inside. Everything was gray. Gray carpet, gray walls, gray ceiling.

"To cut out mental noise," he said, answering the question I was thinking but hadn't asked.

The room was pretty small with a worn sofa against one wall. The other had a four-foot control panel with TV monitors, speakers, and readouts beneath an observation window.

"This is where Stephie sits to monitor my vitals."

"Stephie?"

He motioned to the other room where the girl had greeted us. "I could have anyone I want, but she's pretty hung up on me so I figured why not give her a thrill."

"Lucky her."

"She keeps track of all the stuff when I bilocate."

"Bi . . . locate?"

"When I leave my body and travel."

I tried not to scoff, but he saw my expression.

"What? You don't think I can do it?"

Actually, with everything I'd seen these past few months I figured just about anything was possible. But no way was he going to know it.

He continued, "Maybe you should ask your professor friend. Oh, wait, he's not around any more, is he? Hmm, I wonder where he's gone?"

I bristled. "What do you know about the professor?"

He just grinned that grin of his.

"You know where he is?"

"I only know he was reading up on Dragon

Stealth before he disappeared."

"How do you know that?"

He gave me another one of those, *are-you-really-that-stupid?* looks which made me want to give him another *let-me-rearrange-your-face* makeovers. I settled for grabbing his arm. "Do you think he was . . . could he have been messing with this kinda stuff?" He looked at my grip and I let go.

Then, with a shrug, he answered. "I don't know what he was doing. When I travel, my spirit leaves my body. As far as I can tell, your pal took the whole package with him."

I stood a moment, trying to drink it in.

"C'mon." He turned and I followed him out of the room.

The girl appeared, all smiles. "Here's your coffee." She held out a tray with a couple mugs on it—along with packets of sugar, a spoon, and that girlie-flavored creamer stuff. I nodded a thanks and took a cup.

Chad didn't bother. He left his on the tray, so she had to hold it while he opened the packets, dumped them into his coffee, and poured in the creamer, talking all the while. "This next room here, it's where all the action takes place. We've been working about nine months now and we're already way past whatever those military goons were doing."

"We sure are," Stephie agreed.

He ignored her.

"What about funding?" I asked. "Where are you getting the money?"

"The casinos." He finished stirring the coffee and finally scooped up his mug. "That's what my little visit tonight was about." He motioned me into the other room.

I gave Stephie another nod of thanks but her eyes were too glued to Chad to notice.

The second room was even smaller than the first. Same gray floor, wall, and ceiling. Two recliners, identical to the ones I'd been sketching, in the middle of the room. They were attached to a bunch of sensors and wires.

Once again the kid grinned. "Look familiar? They're ERV chairs."

"ER—"

"Exended Remote Viewing." He moved between them, patting their backs. "Like I said, this is where it all happens. Where I sit during the sessions."

"When you bilocate," I said.

"Very good."

"Two chairs?"

"They originally had two, but I only need one."

"And you're messin' with all this because—?"

"Obviously, because it's a doorway."

"Into . . ."

"Higher dimensions."

The phrase didn't surprise me. We'd been hearing a lot about them . . . and experiencing them. At least according to Littlefoot. Or was she talking about the Multiverse? I shook my head, musing at how I get the terminology mixed up.

"Me, too," he said. "Multiverse, higher dimensions. It can get confusing." I stiffened. He was doing it again, reading my thoughts. "But it'll all make sense when I finally get everything figured out."

"And you, all by yourself, you're going to do that?"

"Of course. But not if I'm standing around

talking to you. So, if you'll excuse me." He turned back to Stephie. "Time to get the show going."

"On it." She hurried away.

"That's it?" I said as he led me out of the room.

"What's it?"

"I take you all the way out here for a thirty second tour?"

"I said from the start I wasn't interested in being recruited. I've got too much on the ball to be held back by rookies. Steph!"

She poked her head around the corner. "Right here."

"Get Belinda a travel cup for the road."

"Will do." She hurried off again.

He gave me a wink. "Can't give away all our dishware to strangers."

"Listen," I kept my voice steady. "I'm not interested in recruiting you. I'm not even interested in being in the same room with you."

"Which is why you're so angry at me for kicking you out."

"Who says I'm angry?"

The kid smiled.

"I'm not angry."

"You're doing a pretty good immitation of it."

I started to answer, then caught myself.

"Super," he said. "Since you're not angry, it'll make goodbyes a lot easier. Steph—"

"Coming." She reappeared with an empty styrofoam cup.

"Give our guest a hand with that," he said.

"Keep it." I set down the mug, none too gently.

"Suit yourself." He turned and stepped back into the second room. "Let's go, Steph. Don't want to waste the entire night."

I headed for the exit, thinking, *unbelievable.*

"Yeah," he called from the other room. "I get that a lot. Stephie?"

"Coming."

Chapter 5

Ninety minutes later Cowboy was glued to the peep-hole in the door of our Preston Towers suite.

"Do you see it?" I asked.

"No ma'am, not yet."

"Good."

"Unless it's out of view," Andi said. She was wrapping a cold towel around my sprained ankle. "The convection of that lens is roughly 190 degrees, leaving 10-20 degrees for an object the size of Brenda's description to hide from view."

"So it could still be out there?" Cowboy asked.

She looked puzzled. "Isn't that what I just said?"

He grinned. "If you say so."

Andi pulled the towel tighter and I tried not to wince. "One thing's for certain," I said, "they know we're here."

"Maybe they followed you from that fella's laboratory, what was his name again?" Cowboy asked.

"Chad." I gritted my teeth against the pain. "Chad Thorton."

Forty minutes earlier, I'd parked the car a few blocks from the hotel and made my way up to the Strip. It was late, but with so many lights you'd swear it was day. Same with the number of people. Youngsters, oldsters, middle-agers. Most had a pretty good buzz going, and 'cept for the belligerent drunk or two, good times were had by all.

Well, almost all.

I didn't see them 'til I entered our hotel and passed through the noisy casino. There were the blurry-eyed smokers playing slots, the studs and students playing tables, and the hostesses delivering drinks. But it was the working girls that tore at me. Youngsters with caked-on makeup trying to look like seasoned vets. Worn-out vets trying to look like youngsters—everyone laughing, joking and flirting . . . and filled with fear, hatred and self-loathing. Memories of another life poured in.

I grabbed a key from the desk and quickly headed for the elevators. I got off on the nineteenth floor. That's when something even more disturbing caught my attention.

A blue metallic orb, about the size of a grapefruit, hovered at the end of the hall. It was exactly like the ones we ran into in Florida and later in LA. We never completely knew what they did, but we did know they belonged to the Gate.

I steeled myself and moved down the hall, pretending not to notice as I headed for the room. I figured it either followed me from Chad Thorton's lab, or someone at the desk had alerted it. Didn't matter. The point was they knew we were here.

I picked up my pace, passed the long line of rooms, including our own, until the stairway at the other end of the hallway came into view. That's when I bolted for the exit. I threw the door open, stepped through, and tried pulling it shut. But no matter how hard I pulled, it took its sweet time closing. I gave up and raced down the stairs as fast as I could. Actually, too fast. When I rounded the landing I rolled my ankle, could actually hear something tear.

I swallowed back the pain and made it to the next floor. I yanked open the door, but knew I couldn't run down the hallway, so I flattened myself against the wall. Just like I figured, the orb shot through the doorway and past me. It flew down the hallway, searching, and I slipped back through the door just before it closed.

I grabbed the railing, pulling myself up one step at a time. I got to the door of our hall, opened it, and limped towards Andi's and my suite. Once I got inside, we called Cowboy. And now here we were, the three of us hiding inside, figuring our next move.

"I say we go into that hallway and face the thing down like we did before," Cowboy said. "Then hightail it out to that fella's place and see what he's up to."

"He's got a point," I said. "We've beat it before."

Andi, who'd had more history with the orbs than us, wasn't so sure. "We were able to do that only with the professor's help," she said.

Of course she was right. At least part right. Which was enough to get me thinking about the old guy again and how much I missed him . . . and wondering if this Chad Thorton had any clues where he might be.

I shook my head at the thought. The last thing I wanted was to go back and put up with his arrogance again. Actually, the second-to-last thing. Facing that orb came in first.

"Mind if I lay hands on it?"

I looked up to see Cowboy staring down at my ankle.

"Knock yourself out," I said. I pulled off the towel. The thing was swollen pretty good. He stooped down and ever so gently wrapped those big paws of his around it. Then he closed his eyes and silently prayed.

Me and Andi watched. More out of respect than any type of faith. Not that we hadn't seen him heal stuff before, but neither of us were as fast at giving God the credit as he was.

After thirty or so seconds, he pulled his hands away. The thing was just as swollen as before.

"Does it feel any better?" he asked.

I tried moving it and winced.

"Sorry," he said.

"Not your fault," I said. "Jesus must got better things to do."

Cowboy nodded, but you could see he wasn't happy about it.

Andi changed subjects. "All right," she said, "this is the pattern I see.

"The orbs are back, which means the Gate is involved and they know we're here."

"Check," Cowboy said.

"This Chad person knows all about the

professor?" she asked.

"A little," I said.

"Enough where he may be able to help?"

I gave a reluctant nod.

"And our sponsors, what did he call them?"

"Watchers," I said

Cowboy frowned. "Kind of a weird name."

"Maybe," Andi said. "But look how they've been keeping an eye on everything since we've started."

"Actually before," I said.

"And helpin' us stop stuff," Cowboy admitted.

Andi continued, "So . . . our sponsors, these Watchers, have clearly sent us here and they've clearly been trying to recruit this man."

"So he says," I said.

Andi pushed back. "He knows too much to be making it up."

"Sometimes more than us," Cowboy said.

I hated it, but they were right.

"So . . ."

Cowboy finished her thought. "We gotta go out there and talk to him."

I groaned.

Andi nodded.

And Cowboy? He turned toward the closed door, preparing himself.

Chapter 6

The good news was there were no floating orbs. Not inside the hotel, not on the Strip. Fact, we got to the car without a single problem with them. But there was another . . .

Since I couldn't drive, Andi had already taken the back seat and Cowboy was helping me into the front. That's when he looked back and asked, "You don't by any chance know them fellas, do you?"

I turned to look and swore. They were the same goons in sunglasses I'd run into before. And they looked just as friendly. "Get in," I ordered. "Hurry."

"Looks like they wanna talk," Cowboy said.

"We gotta go. Now!"

Maybe it was my tone. Maybe it was because they started running toward us. Either way, Cowboy figured it wasn't a bad idea. He crossed to the driver's side and fought to squeeze his giant body behind the wheel. The fact the front seat was broken and wouldn't go back didn't help.

"Hurry!" I yelled. "These guys are serious."

He finally got in, fired up the ignition, and we shot backwards like a rocket.

"You're in reverse!" I shouted.

He ground the gears looking for first. But, like I said, my transmission don't always cooperate. So, still racing backwards and with no other choice, Tank cranked the wheel hard. We missed the car behind us by inches and flew into the street.

Drivers honked, swerved, and cursed. Somehow Cowboy managed to miss them all as the bad guys closed in on us. (Actually we closed in on them). But instead of jumping out of our way, they came straight at us, one from each side.

"Roll up the windows!" Andi yelled.

A nice idea but, again, we're talking my car. The goon on the driver's side got there first. He reached inside and grabbed Cowboy.

"'Scuse me," Cowboy shouted over the roar of the engine, "but yer gonna have to let go."

Before I could point out his good ol' boy manners probably wouldn't help, Goon Two arrived at my side, reached in, and grabbed me.

"Faster!" I shouted to Cowboy.

He punched it. The engine whined and we picked up speed. So did the goons. I don't know if they were running beside us or being dragged. Didn't matter. By the look of things, they weren't letting go.

Cars kept honking and swerving past us. Drivers kept exercising their freedom of speech and hand gestures. And Cowboy kept trying to talk reason to his man. "You're sure makin' it hard to steer this thing," he shouted.

I wasn't so polite. I grabbed the pencil I keep in the cup holder and jabbed it into my guy's face. He yelled and screamed, but still wouldn't let go. So I did it again. Same yelling and screaming, but this time he managed to lose his sunglasses.

That's when I saw he had no eyes. Only empty sockets. Just like those guys in Rome.

"Cowboy!" I shouted.

He glanced over, then yelled, "I thought they looked familiar."

Andi shouted from the back seat. "They're not going to let go! If they're like the others, they'll hang on 'til the end!"

Cowboy nodded, then cranked the wheel hard to the left. We slid our way onto the Strip . . . still going backwards, still drawing irate horns and colorful language.

"Where you going?" I shouted.

"Not sure!" he shouted back. (He was big on honesty).

My guy was still hanging on so I jammed a couple more holes into his face. He yelled and screamed, but still didn't get the message. I glanced over my shoulder and saw we were coming up to our hotel. "Cowboy!"

"Hang on!" he yelled. "I got an idea!"

He swung the car to the right. We bounced up on the curb as pedestrians screamed and jumped out of the way. We headed straight for the front wall, which was mostly glass.

"Cowboy!"

He hit the brakes and we did a perfect 180,

coming to a stop, looking out the windshield at the hotel—complete with bell hops running every direction. But Mr. Toad's wild ride wasn't quite over. Cowboy stomped on the accelerator again.

"Tank!" Andi shouted.

We shot backwards again, this time straight for the street.

"What are you doing?" I yelled.

He motioned to the two giant hitching posts in front of the hotel. The ones spaced as wide apart as my car. Well, almost.

"Just scrapin' off the barnacles!" he shouted. Hang on!"

We flew between the posts and did exactly what he'd hoped . . . removed the unwanted debris, leaving the bad guys in a groaning heap on the sidewalk. In exchange, the sound of scraping metal told me I'd also acquired a racing stripe the length of my car.

"Where'd you learn that?" Andi shouted.

"Barrel racing." He grinned. "I used to do rodeo as a kid."

Chapter 7

"This the place?" Cowboy asked as he crawled out of the car and crossed to my side.

"This is it."

Once he helped me to my feet I got a healthy look at the gouge running from my front fender to my back bumper.

"Sorry about that," he said.

The good news was he'd gotten my car out of reverse. The bad news was it got us to Chad Thorton's.

It's not that I didn't like the kid, it's just—all right. I didn't like him . . . a lot. I didn't like his arrogance. I didn't like how he treated his assistant. And I didn't like him calling us amateurs, particularly after all we'd been through.

"Look," Andi said as she got to the door. "A

note. It's addressed to a Belinda."

"Give that to me." I ripped it down and read:

> *Welcome back. Come in if you must.*
> *But don't disturb. Our work is too*
> *vital.*

"Wow," Cowboy said, reading over my shoulder. "He sounds important."

I crumpled the paper and tossed it to the ground.

Instead of knocking, I pushed at the door. It opened and we stepped inside. Everything was like before, except for the flute and harp music playing in the background. And the two rooms. Both of their doors were shut.

"Where is everybody?" Cowboy whispered.

I limped to the little square window in the door of the observation room. The girl, Stephie, sat at the console in her white stocking cap. I tapped the glass. She looked up, grinned, and motioned for us to come in, but quietly.

We entered, all reverent, like in a funeral home. Once introductions were whispered, she turned back to the console and window looking into the other room. Chad sat in one of the recliners, all sorts of wires and sensors attached to him.

"Is he sleeping?" Cowboy asked.

Stephie shook her head. "Traveling." She glanced up at the digital clock above the window. It read:

02:59:38

"Almost three hours now."

"Traveling?" Andi asked.

33

"Bilocating." Stephie looked at me, a question on her face like I should have already told them. I shook my head and she continued. "It's a fairly simple technique where you train your phantom body to leave your physical body.

"Lucid dreaming," Andi said.

"In a fashion."

Andi nodded. "There have been multiple studies on the practice. Not always favorable."

Stephie continued, "Unlike lucid dreaming, bilocation occurs when the subject is fully awake." She pressed what must have been an intercom button and spoke, "Coming up to three hours." She looked at the clock, waiting until it clicked over to:

03:00:00

"And mark: Three hours."

"How is that possible?" Andi asked. "While being awake?"

"It takes several months of training—learning to merge the brainwaves of the left and right hemispheres, using various biofeedback techniques to lower breathing and heart rates, dropping brain waves from beta to alpha until they finally reach the target state, which would be theta activity."

I was impressed at how smart and confident she sounded when Chad wasn't around.

"Chad told me it used to be an Army program?" I said.

"That's right. They would find gifted individuals and train them to bilocate—send their phantom bodies into enemy installations and spy on top secret operations."

"When you say phantom bodies, is that like their souls?" Cowboy asked.

Stephie shrugged. "Call it what you like. Either way, the results were quite accurate."

"You said, 'gifted' individuals?'" Andi asked.

"That's right. People like Chad, here. Or," she motioned to me, "Belinda."

"Brenda," I corrected her.

"Really? Because he said it was—"

"Trust me, it's Brenda."

"By *gifted*," Andi said, "what do you mean?"

"People who have a natural psychic ability." She nodded to me. "Like the drawings Chad says you draw. I imagine your psychic rating is quite—"

"She ain't no psychic," Cowboy said.

We turned to him. He was doing his best to be polite, but wasn't quite pulling it off. "Miss Brenda here, her gift is prophetic, like in the Bible. Not psychic. That's occult."

Stephie frowned. "I fail to see the difference."

"Trust me, ma'am, it's a big difference. One is a gift from God, the other, it's a counterfeit used to trick and trap people into—"

"I'm in." Chad's voice came from the console speaker. I looked through the window. His eyes were closed and he seemed totally relaxed, but it was definitely him doing the talking.

Stephie hit the intercom switch. "What do you see?"

"The usual snow. Lots of it."

She scooted to a nearby keyboard and began typing as he continued.

"Same mountains. Everything's the same."

"And the wall?" she asked.

"I'm approaching it now. Seems a lot colder today."

Stephie glanced at another readout. "Your skin temperature is 89.9." She leaned closer to the window. "I see goosebumps on your arms."

"I should have worn a coat."

"Is that possible?" I asked. "Goosebumps?"

She answered while checking other readouts. "There has to be some connection between his phantom and physical body."

"Or?"

"Or he'd be dead."

His voice came back through the speaker. "Still no opening. Still no way to access—wait. What the—"

"Problem?" she asked.

"There's a giant triangle. Can't make out its composition, but it's floating five, six hundred meters above me and to the right. The thing is huge, like an ocean liner and—" He sucked in his breath. "It spotted me. It spotted me and is heading directly for me."

"Chad, get out of there. Now."

"Wait. Something's got hold of me. Nothing physical but . . . like a force field or something."

"Chad?"

No answer.

"Chad, answer me! Chad, I'm ending the session."

"No," he gasped, "too dangerous."

"Dangerous?" I asked.

She answered without looking. "Shock to his limbic system. The transition has to be gentle. And self-initiated. Too abrupt and it could break the connection, his vitals could shut down, go into cardiac arr—"

"It's okay. I'm free." You could hear the strain in his voice, see his chest heaving up and down. "Now if I can just hide behind this outcropping."

Stephie called out another reading. "Heart rate 182. BP is—"

"There. Good. Okay, I'm coming home."

And then silence.

"Chad . . .

More silence.

I looked to Stephie. She waited, nervously watching the clock. Tens seconds. Fifteen. We all figured it was better not to talk.

At twenty seconds, she hit the intercom again. "Chad, can you hear me. Chad, do you—"

He began gasping for breath.

"Chad—"

Suddenly his eyes popped open. He blinked, then lifted his head and looked through the window, grinning.

"You're back!" Stephie cried.

Still breathing hard, he answered, "Of course I'm back." He spotted me and our little group standing beside her. "So the pupil has returned to the teacher, has she? Oh, and look, she's brought her pals."

Chapter 8

"The Gate?" Andi asked incredulously. "You were at the headquarters of the Gate?"

"Their wall, yeah." Chad didn't bother swallowing his mouthful of eggs. "You want to pass those hash browns here? These little excursions leave me starved."

Cowboy, who'd put away a fair amount of breakfast himself, passed the platter up the table.

It had been a long night. The sun was just peeking over the mountains. Stephie had thrown together a pretty impressive breakfast—unnoticed by Chad, but appreciated by the rest of us. We were eating outside, enjoying the few minutes of cool air before the desert heated up. Well, Cowboy and Chad were eating. Stephie was flitting about the table making sure we were all happy (*we* as in Chad)—while me and Andi nibbled here and there, carefully listening.

The kid continued, doing his best to impress Andi. At twenty-two, he was three or four years her junior. But it didn't stop him from making the moves. Moves she was either too polite to comment on or too naive to notice. Didn't matter. If Boy Wonder was trolling, me and Cowboy would make sure he got both arms broken before reeling her in. "It's their headquarters," he said, "at least here on earth. Or above it."

I frowned.

"From what I've been able to hear, they have plenty more."

We all traded looks, rememberin' Littlefoot's comments during our last outing.

"You've seen 'em?" Cowboy asked.

He shook his head. "Just heard their thoughts."

"And you think they're from another planet," I said.

"Another universe," Andi corrected.

I nodded. "Right, another universe?"

"For starters, yeah. But from what I can tell, there's something more."

"More?" I said.

"We're talking another dimension. Maybe several."

We traded looks some more.

Andi cleared their throat. "You say you've heard their conversations?"

He looked at her and smiled. "Yeah, lots of

times." He gave a little stretch. "Not that I'm one to brag—"

"Since when?" I muttered.

"—but with my gift it's pretty easy to hear what they're thinking. And believe me, sweet cheeks, you folks better worry, because they're thinking a lot."

Andi ignored the flirt and said, "I thought you didn't care what they were thinking, that you weren't interested in stopping them."

"I'm not."

"Then . . ."

"I'm just interested in the money."

"How's that work?" I said.

"Easy. I sell you information. You pass it on to the Watchers. I walk away rich and safe."

"Safe 'cause you're not taking sides," I said.

"Safe's important." He turned to Cowboy. "Which explains that AK-47 you've been wondering about at my front door."

Cowboy's jaw slacked. "How did you know I was thinking . . ." He slowed to a stop as the kid tapped his temple. The big fellow scowled, not liking it one bit.

"And how do we know the information you'll offer is correct?" Andi asked.

"Because I'm never wrong."

"I'll be sure to tell Belinda that," I said.

He smiled. "I'm never wrong about important issues."

"And how do we know we can trust you?" Andi said.

He turned his gaze on her, getting all Barry White. "Because I never lie to people I'm attracted to. Or to those who find me attractive."

I cut in. "And the professor. You've seen him?"

"Maybe."

I scoffed. "How much they supposed to pay for *maybe*?"

Stephie, who was making the rounds with a pitcher of orange juice, came to his defense. "Everything Chad's seen has been carefully recorded. We keep very good logs."

Chad ignored her and leaned across the table to me. "What if I were to show you?"

"Show me what?"

"Like I said, you have a little bit of the gift. Pathetically small, I'll grant you, but you still have it."

"I'm flattered."

"You have enough for me to at least take you for a little spin."

I felt myself stiffen, but managed to look calm. I think.

He turned back to Andi. "And you, there's so much you could learn by watching. By just staying at my side."

"Me?"

"Of course. I can always use another assistant. The more the merrier."

The pitcher slipped from Stephie's hand, crashing to the table. "Gracious me, I'm so sorry." She grabbed a napkin and started mopping up.

I barely noticed. Not because of Chad's flirting or his out-of-control ego. But because of the offer. What if I really could connect with the professor? What if there really was a way to discover the Gate's headquarters?

I turned back to him. "How long would it take?"

"For what?"

He was dangling the bait, but I had to play along. "How long would it take to get me ready for something like that?"

"With me as your teacher? I'd say . . ." He gave us a dramatic pause, then answered: "Now."

I caught my breath.

"If you have the nerve."

I closed my mouth, gave the muscles in my jaw a workout. He was setting the hook all right, there was no doubt about it. And we both knew I had no choice but to swallow it.

"Miss Brenda?"

I looked to Cowboy.

"I don't think that's a very good idea."

"Because?" Chad asked.

"Because it's the occult. You're playing with things you don't understand."

"And you people do?" Chad asked.

"I understand what's forbidden."

"According to?"

"The Bible."

It was the kid's turn to scoff. "Too bad your professor the Bible scholar didn't get that memo."

"You really think she could see the professor?" Andi asked.

"Maybe. Who knows? Like I said to—" he paused, pretending he was trying to remember my name—"Brenda here; the man was definitely researching our stuff." He turned back to me. "I can't promise you the professor, but I can take you to the Gate. At least its perimeter, the one here on Earth."

I felt my ears beginning to burn. Heard the faint pounding of my heart.

"Miss Brenda?" It was Cowboy again. Doing his

best to warn me.

The kid cocked his head sideways, all coy-like. "Well?"

I took the slightest breath to steady myself, then gave the answer. "Of course."

Chapter 9

"Heartbeat's at forty-eight." Stephie's voice came through the speaker of our room, all soft and gentle. "You can bring it lower than that."

I took a deep breath, trying to relax.

"Don't *try* to relax," Boy Wonder said. He was stretched out in the recliner beside me, talking like he was reading my mind, which he probably was. "Just let it happen."

"Approaching theta," Stephie said. "That's good, very good."

People, they call me a control freak. They're probably right. I been 'round too much to let some stranger call the shots. Even well-meaning, white chicks trying to use their hocus-pocus hypno-voice on me.

"But she's trying to help," the kid answered.

Will you stop that! I thought.

"Oops," Stephie said, "you're back up to alpha."

I took another breath. I tried focusing on the soft flute music playing in the background, imagined myself melting into the recliner.

"That's better. Good, good. Keep breathing, nice and slow. In and out. In and out. A little more. Good. And . . . we're there."

For being *there*, I felt exactly the same. Except, well, gradually, I noticed it was like I didn't have any arms and legs. And that I was falling. Falling through darkness. Except it wasn't all dark. There was some sort of tunnel around me. On all sides. And I wasn't falling down, I was floating up.

Where am I? I spoke or thought or both.

"Just go with it," Chad said.

I heard wind begin blowing in my ears. Faint at first, but it got pretty loud pretty fast. I actually felt it on my face. That's when the lights or stars or whatever they were started going by. Slow at first, but they picked up speed 'til they were streaking past me, blurring by like one of those Star War movies. And with all that blurring I started seeing faces on the tunnel walls. Actually the walls *were* the faces, some small, some big, most creepy like those gargoyles you see on top of buildings.

Like the ones I'd sketched on my pad.

Do you see me? It was Chad's voice again. I couldn't tell if it was inside my head or out.

I don't—

Focus on the center of the tunnel. Away from the faces.

In my mind, I pretended to squint, looking hard

until . . . there, fifty yards away. Chad was standing waving his arms at me.

I see you. I see someone.

Of course you do. As usual he was talking down to me like I was a kid. But suddenly things changed. His voice and image rippled like a wave. They did it again, faster. And faster. 'Til everything was a blur, just rippling colors and sound.

Chad! Chad, You there?

No answer. Just the flowing colors and sounds. Then the sound of birds. Then voices—a boy and a girl. The colors began taking shape. Patches of blue sky. White, puffy clouds. Tree tops. Then roofs, then porches, front yards. Not ghetto, but lower class. I looked down to see I was standing on an uneven sidewalk, weeds growing between the cracks.

The voices got clearer.

I turned to see the two kids just a few feet away, twelve, maybe thirteen-years-old. A pretty girl in a print blouse and cutoffs. She was doing most of the talking. Arguing, really. And the boy? No doubt. Don't ask me how, but I knew it was a younger version of Chad Thorton, complete with cracking voice.

"Melissa, please. You gotta understand—"

"You ruined my grade! You ruined everything!" The girl pretended to cry, but it was obviously fake. Not that Chad could tell. The boy was a newbie when it came to drama queens.

He tried explaining. "I, I didn't want to do it in the first place. It's cheating and that's wrong, but—"

"You gave me wrong questions for the test and you blame me?"

"No one's blaming—"

"You said you could read Mrs. Snider's mind. You said you could tell me what she'd ask."

"I said I'd try."

"You're such a loser. Everyone says so."

He tried to hide the pain filling his face.

"A freak. That's what they say. Freak!"

"Melis—"

"I should have listened." Before he answered, she repeated: "Freak!" Then turned and ran off.

"Melissa?" You could hear his anguish. And unlike the girl, you could see his tears were real. "Melissa . . ."

I wanted to say something, but doubted he could hear or see me.

His face rippled in another wave. Trees and houses blurred back to colors and light. The ground shook under my feet. Only it wasn't ground. Other faces appeared. All around me. Then seats and walls . . . of a school bus. I was standing inside a moving school bus.

Kids were shouting and laughing. Pushing and shoving to see out the windows on one side. I joined them—surprised, but not scared when I passed through them like they were pockets of air.

I got to the windows. There, at the top of a flagpole, a pair of jockey underwear was flapping in the breeze. But that wasn't what the kids were laughing at. It was the sixteen-year-old who was tied to the bottom of the pole, buck naked, trying to cover his privates. Chad Thorton.

My face grew hot. No one should have to go through that. Particularly a teen. Not even if that teen happened to be wonder boy. I turned and pushed my way through to the front of the bus. I'd barely stepped out before the picture blurred and disappeared. Along with the laughing and jeering. Now there was another voice. Smaller. Helpless.

"Daddy? Daddy, please. I'll be good."

Bits and pieces of a different picture appeared. A closed door. A crack of light under it.

"Daddy . . ."

And the smell. Urine. And worse. Like someone had taken a dump right there in . . . in a closet. I was standing in a closet. Next to me, huddled against a wall, legs pulled in, whimpering, was a little boy, five-years-old—maybe younger. Another version of Chad Thorton.

"Daddy, please, I'll be good, I promise . . ."

Next to the crack under the door was a dog dish, its bowl barely filled with water.

"Daddy . . ."

Suddenly I heard popping. Outside, but close. Fast and rapid. Adrenalin surged through my body. I know gunfire when I hear it. With that realization, came the weight returning to my arms, my legs. Then the pressure of the recliner, the sensors around my chest and arms, the restraints.

"Chad? Brenda?" It was Stephie's voice. "You two need to come back. Guys . . ."

I pried open my eyes. I was back in the room. I turned to see Chad.

More gun fire. Automatic.

I tried speaking. "What's—" My voice was thick and hoarse. I tried again. "What's happening?"

"An attack," Chad said as he began unhooking his monitors. "We're under attack."

Chapter 10

It took me a minute to unhook the monitors and get off the restraints. Stephie was still in the observation room, shutting stuff down. Cowboy and Andi were already outside. Not Chad. Boy Wonder had left me behind only to get as far as the front door where he refused to step out.

"What's goin' on?" I shouted as I ran toward him.

"The spheres!" he yelled. "They're back."

I reached the door and looked past him. Not far from my car floated Cowboy. He was fifteen feet above the ground. Around him, forming the corners of a clear box, were not one of the orbs, but eight. Each about ten feet from the other. And, though you could barely see them in the daylight, there were walls stretching between 'em. Six walls, forming a prison with Cowboy inside: a ten-by-ten foot cube he couldn't get out of.

"Cowboy!"

"Shh." Chad took a half step behind the door. "They'll hear you."

I gave him a scowl.

"He'll be okay," he said.

"Okay? They got him locked up in some sort of box."

"He started it."

"What?"

"See those two on the ground?"

I looked back outside and spotted two more orbs. They were in the dirt, ripped apart and smoldering.

"And that?" He motioned to the AK-47 lying on the ground. "Looks like he shot them down."

I swore and started out the door. Chad caught my arm. "You have no idea what they can do."

"Yeah." I shook him off and stepped outside. "I do."

Cowboy saw me and shouted, pounded on the walls, trying to warn me. I couldn't hear him. Didn't matter if I could.

Andi thought the same. She stood out there, not far away, hands on her hips shouting up at them. "Put him down! Put him down this instant!" Granted, it wasn't her best plan, or her brightest. But it was vintage Andi. Don't let her southern politeness fool you. When it came to protecting the rest of our team, she was one mother of a momma bear.

The orbs ignored her. Me, too. They obviously needed more convincing. So I headed for the rifle. I barely got there and scooped it up 'fore they figured what I was up to. Suddenly, the whole cube, Cowboy and all, began spinning . . . and coming straight at me. I didn't even get the gun raised before one of the corner orbs knocked it out of my hand.

The next one knocked me to the ground.

And the next one?

Well there was no next, 'cause suddenly I was inside the cube with Cowboy. The walls still spun, but we hung inside, pretty much stationary. There was so much wind I couldn't hear a thing. But I could see. Andi stood right below us, shouting and carrying on. Until the cube started toward her.

But she still wouldn't back down.

Then, just before we swallowed her up to join the party, my car window blew to pieces. Glass flying everywhere.

Then my side mirror.

Then my left front tire.

I turned and spotted Stephie. She'd raced outside, picked up the gun and was firing away. I appreciated the effort, though she wasn't exactly the best of shots. Still, what she lacked in skill, she made up with enthusiasm. Bullets flew everywhere and in every direction.

Our whirling cube changed direction. Instead of going after Andi, it went after Stephie. But the girl kept firing away, looking like the star in some old Rambo movie. Then, somehow, don't ask me how, she actually got one. The orb exploded into a ball of sparks and fell to the ground.

Without it, one of our walls fizzled and disappeared. And since the cube was still spinning we got thrown out, sailed through the air, and landed a dozen feet away.

And Stephie? She just kept shootin'. Eventually,

she hit another one, that exploded and fell. The cube, which had been wobbling from losing the first orb, went completely out of control. It spun and tumbled every which way until it slammed into the ground, bounced, smashed into my car (leaving a healthy dent at the end of my racing stripe), crashed back to the ground, and then flew apart.

But only for a second. 'Cause the orbs came back together again, forming a tight little circle. They hovered there like they were trying to make up their minds.

Stephie helped them decide by firing a dozen more rounds—mostly into my car. Still, the orbs got the message. They shot straight up into the sky, faster than anything I'd ever seen, 'til they were completely out of sight.

Everything got real quiet. Me and Cowboy, we struggled to our feet, checking for bruises and broken body parts. Andi, too. And Stephie? She looked as surprised at what she'd done as the rest of us. Which explains why she stared at the rifle a moment before throwing it to the ground.

That's when I heard my cell buzzing. I pulled it from my pocket and saw it was a text message from Daniel. It read:

Are you okay?

I shook my head, once again amazed at his timing. Even though my fingers were shaking I managed to type back:

Yes. You?

I barely finished before his second half came in.

You have to get out of there.
Something bad is coming.
Real bad.

I frowned and was about to answer when I heard Chad's voice.

"We all good?" He stood outside the door, hands in his pockets, looking like nothing ever happened. And it hadn't. At least to him. "Well, will you look at that car."

He strolled up to it . . . shattered window, broken mirror, blown out tire, giant crater, and the steady dribble of water which could only come from my radiator.

"Don't want to be a downer, but it looks like you may be stuck here a while."

Chapter 11

When I was a kid, going twenty-four hours with no sleep wasn't a big deal. But now? Forget it. I barely hit the pillow before I was out. In this case that would be Stephie's pillow.

"You just make yourself comfortable," she'd said. "You've had a long day."

"What about you?"

"I've got some tools in the side shed. Let me see what I can do for that radiator of yours. Looks like it just might be a hose."

I'd like to think she was just bein' helpful, and maybe she was. But I'm guessing some of it had to do with keeping an eye on Chad, not to mention getting

Andi out of there as soon as possible. Not that he'd have a chance with Andi. But to protect her interests, I understand that a girl's gotta do what a girl's gotta do.

Still, whatever she saw in him was beyond me.

Okay, I admit maybe I'd started feeling a little sorry for him, considering what I'd seen in his past—the bullying and all that abuse. And yeah, that probably explains him being such a jerk. But it was going to take more than that to forgive him for being the coward hiding behind the door.

Course he had his excuses which he'd been only too happy to share later, around the table. "It's obvious I'm the one they were after. Considering all I've been accomplishing."

"Don't know about that," I said. "They seemed pretty interested in Cowboy, here."

"Only because he drew their attention with the gun." Leaning past Cowboy, he spoke to Andi. "Would you be a doll and go ask Stephie to get us some more coffee?"

Andi's response—narrowing her gaze and ignoring him—made me proud of her. I got back to the question at hand. The one that had been needling me. "What happened when we were bilocating?"

"You mean the Timefold thing?" he said.

"Is that what you call it?"

"That's what I call it."

"I didn't exactly make it to the Gate's headquarters."

"Yeah, sometimes that happens," he said. "I wondered where you went."

"So it was real?"

"What did you see?"

"Mostly you as a kid. Like when they tied you to the flag pole naked."

"You saw that?"

I nodded. "And when, it must have been your old man, when he locked you in the closet with just a dog's bowl for water and—"

"Right, right," he cut me off. "Time folding."

"So you traveled back in time?" Andi asked.

"In a manner of speaking." He called toward the kitchen door. "Steph? How's that coffee coming?"

"I'll be there in a jiffy," came the voice

He turned back to us. "When we bilocate, we leave behind our three dimensional world and enter a higher dimension."

"The spirit world," Cowboy said.

"If that's what you want to call it, sure. And right next to that dimension is another. Time."

"I thought time was supposed to be the fourth dimension," I said.

He looked at me, musing. "It would be nice if things were that tidy, wouldn't it? Let alone, stable. But as you've experienced, that's not always the case."

"True," Cowboy said. "We've had some pretty crazy adventures."

"Right. Whatever. Stephie!"

So now I'm in Stephie's room, trying to get some sleep. The sleep came, no problem. Not the rest.

Maybe it was Daniel's warning: *Something bad is coming. Real bad.* Or Cowboy's uneasiness about psychics. Or the frog-faced gremlins I'd seen along the edges of the tunnel.

They're what haunted me the most. Seems every time I closed my eyes and drifted off, they were there. On Stephie's walls, her ceiling. Some even on the bed.

For the most part I was able to ignore them. Just tellin' myself they were a dream.

Until a couple of them jumped on my chest.

I actually thought I could feel their weight, like they were makin' it hard to breathe. I tried to shout, but nothing came. I tried to move, but it was like I was paralyzed. When I opened my eyes they were inches from my face, leering down at me. I gasped, tried again to scream.

Nothing came but a croaking cry.

They moved closer to my lips. I clamped my mouth tight, my nostrils flaring, trying to get enough air. I tried screaming again. A pathetic whimper.

"Miss Brenda? Miss Brenda, wake up." I turned and there was Cowboy, kneeling on the floor beside me. "You okay?"

I raised my head and looked. They were gone.

I took a deep breath.

"Are you okay?"

I took another breath and nodded. "Just a bad dream, that's all."

He looked at me skeptically.

"I'm all right. Really."

"Hmm," was all he said. Then, without a word, he turned and, still on the floor, rested his back against the mattress.

"What are you doing?" I said.

"Jus' staying here . . . case you have another one."

Chapter 12

"Brenda?" Somebody was shaking me . . . again.

I pried open one eye to see Andi staring down at me. "'Sup?" I muttered.

"It's Chad. We've got a problem."

"You think?" I tried turning over, but she stopped me.

"I'm serious."

"What's going on?" Cowboy, who'd fallen asleep on my floor, was doing his own imitation of trying to sound coherent.

"Chad." The fear in Andi's voice told me it was going to be impossible to go back to sleep. "He needs our help."

A minute or two later we were all crowding into the room with the recliners. Stephie was there, doing everything she could to pull Chad out of his trance or whatever he was in. He was all hooked up and strapped into the recliner like before, but this time his body was jerking like he was having some sort of seizure.

"Chad!" She shook him. "Can you hear me?"

An alarm was sounding in the Observation Room.

"What's wrong?" Andi said.

"He's gone."

"He's what?

"He tried coming back, but something—I don't know. Chad!"

"How often does this happen?" Andi asked.

"Chad!"

"Stephie?" Andi repeated.

"Never."

"You sayin' he *can't* come back or he won't?" I said.

"Chad, can you hear me?"

"Can't or won't?"

"Can't. And the longer he stays—" She couldn't finish and started shaking him again.

"There's got to be somethin' you can do?" Cowboy said.

"Not out here."

"Out here?" Andi asked.

"It has to be from inside. Someone has to join him from the inside—help him out from in there."

"So do it," Cowboy said.

"Not me. It has to be someone with the ability. Someone with experience who can . . ."

She came to a stop and turned to me.

I looked away.

"Someone with the ability?" Andi repeated.

"Yes. Someone who can—"

His body gave a violet jerk. If it wasn't for the restraints he'd have flown out of the chair.

"Chad!" Stephie cried.

His mouth opened like he was trying to scream, but only choking sounds came out.

Andi looked at me. "Brenda?"

I pretended not to hear. I knew exactly what she was thinking and no way was I going back in there, wherever "there" was. Especially for the likes of him.

Another alarm sounded from the Observation Room. Shriller than the other.

"He's going into v-fib!" Stephie yelled. She began ripping off his sensors, fighting with the one wrapped around his chest. "Give me a hand!"

Cowboy obliged, holding down Chad's bucking body, which freed Stephie to struggle with the sensors.

"A crash cart?" Andi shouted. "Do you have a defibrillator?"

Stephie shook her head as she tore open his shirt. "Too expensive. Said we didn't need it."

I stared down at him as he continued to fight and gasp. Then I heard a voice:

"Daddy . . ." It didn't come from him, but from the little boy locked in the closet. I looked around. Nobody else heard it. *"Daddy, I'll be good."*

Stephie thumped on his bare chest. Then again. And again.

Nothing. Except . . .

It was no longer his body she pounded. It was the chest of the naked teen, arms stretched out to a flag pole. The boy's cries were drowned out by older kids —laughing, mocking.

"Brenda?"

I blinked, turned to see Andi looking at me.

I shook my head. "No!"

Another alarm began.

"He's flat-lining!" Stephie cried. She shoved the heel of her palm against his chest and began pumping with both hands, giving him CPR.

Only it wasn't him. Or the teenage kid. It was the twelve-year-old version. I still heard the crowd jeering, the little boy crying, but now I saw and heard the twelve-year-old pleading with the girl:

"Melissa . . ."

"You're such a loser. Everyone says so."

"What are you doing?" I looked up to see Andi shouting to Cowboy.

He glanced up from his cell. "Calling 911."

"They'll never make it!" Stephie cried as she continued to pump. "We're too far!" She threw another look to me.

"Daddy, please, Daddy, I'll be good. The laughter was louder. So was the girl, *"Freak. That's what they say. Freak!"*

"Brenda?" Andi asked again.

The images returned, repeated themselves. The naked teen. The twelve-year-old. The kid locked in the closet.

"Daddy, I'll be good."

"Freak!

The laughter grew to a roar, the voices screaming

over it,

"Daddy!
Freak!
I'll be good.
Everybody says—
Daddy, please—
Freak!
Daddy I'll be—
Freak—
Dad—"

"All right!" I shouted. "All right!"

Cowboy looked up at me.

But Stephie got it. So did Andi.

"Get her into the other chair," Stephie ordered. "Quickly."

Andi said, "Will she be in any danger?"

"Not much. I don't know. Hurry!"

Chapter 13

The voices still screamed in my head as I flew through the tunnel. Maybe they were in my head, maybe they weren't, who knows? Add to that my snarling, toad-faced friends stuck to the side of the walls, and it was quite a party.

I was coming up to the end of the tunnel and saw what looked like a blizzard—blowing snow, wind growing stronger by the second.

"Looks like a snow storm," I said, or thought, or both.

Stephie answered. "You're approaching the end of the portal. Any sign of Chad?"

"I hear his voices, but don't see anything."

"Follow them. Follow the voices. Chances are they'll lead you to him. But slow down. Start walking."

"I'm flying. How am I supposed to—"

"In your imagination. Think yourself heavy, so heavy you're falling to your feet."

It made no sense. But nothing else did, either, so I gave it a try. I pretended I was big; Jabba-the-Hut big. And it worked. Immediately my feet touched down and I started walking. But I'd only taken a step or two before the whole tunnel disappeared. Now I was surrounded by giant, snow-covered cliffs on every side. And icy wind that cut through my shirt.

"You in the mountains, yet?"

"Yeah, how did you—"

"The Gate's headquarters. This is where we've been going for days. Do you see the wall?"

"Nothing. Just rocks and snow and—wait a minute." Directly in front of me I spotted something flat and coated in snow. It stretched out in every direction as far as I could see.

"What is it? What do you see?"

I reached out and gently touched it. It was freezing. "Some sort of surface," I said. "Flat and smooth."

"The wall. Good. He's got to be around there somewhere."

I pressed harder to get a better feel. That's when my fingers disappeared.

"What the—" I pulled back my hand and my fingers returned.

"What's wrong? What happened?"

I reached out again, hesitated, then pressed the

wall again. Same thing. I pushed harder, felt the wind blow against my hand, then my wrist. Just like moving through those kids in the school bus. I pulled my hand out. Checked it. Everything looked good.

"Brenda? What's happening?"

I tried again, this time shoving my whole arm through and pulling it out. Still no problem.

"Brenda?"

I stuck both arms into it. Same thing, which I figured was good enough. I closed my eyes, clenched my jaw and inched forward. The puff of air hit my chest, then my face, and then—

"Bren—"

The snow was gone. The cold too. I was floating again. This time in front of a giant window. One that looked down on, and I know this sounds crazy, but I was looking down on the Earth. It was small, 'bout the size of a soccer ball, with a thin haze around it. And stars. Hundreds, thousands of them. Really breathtaking. And tranquil. Except for the laughter. And the voices:

I'll be good. Everybody says—Daddy. Melissa, please—Freak! Daddy I'll be— Freak! Dad—

They were coming from behind me, louder than ever. I turned and caught my breath. There were thousands of floating snowflakes. Beautiful. Each one just a little bigger than a man. Not flat, but round like globes. And they were growing. Large crystals kept forming along their edges making them bigger and bigger. And in each crystal was a scene, like a 3-D movie. Hundreds of them playing at once. More being added by the minute.

"You guys won't believe this," I said.

But there was no answer.

"Hello? Stephie, can you hear me?"

Still nothing. Just the laughter and the voices.

Using my imagination, like I did in the tunnel, I willed myself toward the sound. It worked. I began drifting past one snowflake then another. Just like real snowflakes, each one was different. Each one growing and showing different scenes.

Except, up ahead . . .

One had three children floating around it—actually, on one side of it. Their hands were stretched out and no crystals were growing in that direction. The other sides grew just fine, but the ones closest to the kids' hands had stopped. So, as the snowflake got bigger, it kept getting more and more lopsided. Instead of being beautiful, it was becoming more and more deformed.

The kids must have sensed my presence 'cause all three slowly turned. Goosebumps popped up on my arms. And it had nothing to do with the cold. It was their eyes. They were totally black. Just like the kids we'd seen in Florida.

I gave them a wide birth, and kept following the voices:

Melissa, please—Freak! Daddy I'll be—

Finally, I arrived at their source. There was no mistaking it. Somehow, someway this snowflake had to do with Chad Thorton. Not only were the voices the loudest here, but I could actually see a scene of his life playing in the closest crystal. The scene of him hiding behind the door during our fight with the orbs. Beside it was another crystal. This one showing us having breakfast outside with him behind the lab.

"Stephie?" I shouted. "Guys?"

Still no answer.

Carefully, I reached out and touched the outer crystal. It was frosty and cold, just like the wall. So I pressed harder and my hand passed through, just like with the wall.

Except, I couldn't pull it out. Instead, something powerful grabbed my wrist. It yanked me hard. So hard that before I knew it, I'd fallen inside the giant snowflake.

Chapter 14

I wasn't lying when I said the snowflakes were 'bout the size of a man. But once I was inside Chad's, I kept falling, going deeper and deeper. And the deeper I went, the more I could see the crystals around me, each one playing a different scene. Things like me driving him to the lab, being chased by the eyeless goons, slamming into him with my car. The deeper I fell, the farther back in his life the scenes went.

Pretty soon I was surrounded by his college years, awkward and nerdy. Even worse were his high school scenes, including the guys stripping him and tying him to the flagpole. Middle school wasn't much better, full of pimples, porn, and, of course, Melissa shutting him down. Finally there were the fights, beatings really, when he was younger. Seemed every wannabe bully practiced on him . . . including his old man.

Then the scenes stopped. As best I could tell I'd reached the center. No more crystals. Just Chad, full grown, on his knees and crying like a baby. Instead of crystals, he was surrounded by shadows. Big ones towering over him. But, as far as I could tell, nothing was making them. They were only shadows, places where the light just sort of vanished.

I called to him. "Chad?"

He looked up, face wet with tears.

"Can you hear me?"

He cocked his head like he heard something. Peered like he was trying to see. But it was obvious he couldn't see through the darkness.

"It's me!" I said.

"Brenda?"

"We gotta get you out of here. Your body, back in the lab, it's—"

"They've caught me. I'm trapped."

"By what? Those things? They're just shadows." I started towards him.

"No! Don't come any closer. It's not safe."

"I didn't come all the way here to be run off by shadows. Now come on, we gotta get you—"

"Go back. Warn the others."

He was starting to piss me off. "They're just shadows. Let's go!" I stepped into the first one. "Let's—" And it hit me. Everything at once. Memories so clear it was like I was there . . .

I'm seven years old, shoplifting Hello Kitty pencils. Other stuff flickers past. Embarrassing stuff.

Shameful. I'm nine years old, giving in to my step-dad, letting him do his thing. Again. And again. Now I'm beating up Jimmy McPherson, torturing the neighbor's cat, breaking school windows. I feel the shadow seeping into me. Icy cold. More stuff. Things I've tried forgetting . . .

Making out with my seventh grade teacher. Doing it with Boyd on the living room floor, Johnson in his Mustang, smoking weed, giving up baby Monique, the meth, breaking into homes. My stomach is turning. I want to puke. I can't catch my breath.

The first abortion. Cussing out Mom. My botched suicide. Her tears sponging up the blood from the bathroom tiles, the second abortion, the DUI's, jail . . .

I begin to sob. Can't help myself. My knees are getting weak. I lower to the ground. No light around me now. Only the shadows. Darkness. And more memories . . .

The dealing. Sex for money. More men than I can count, Caroline's OD, working the Strip. Everything is hopeless. No way out.

When suddenly there is a roar, like a waterfall. The memories shimmer, then break apart. Someone is touching my shoulder. I look up. There's a small patch of light. In it I see the old nun, the one who helped us back in Italy.

"Help . . ." my voice came out as a raspy whisper.

She understood. She took my arm and helped me to my feet. And suddenly . . . the shadows were gone. I could see them, feel them all around me, but they weren't in me, they weren't on me.

"Brenda . . . are you there?"

I turned to Chad. He was just feet away and still

covered in dark. The old lady raised her arm. It wasn't much. A small gesture. But suddenly there was a ripping sound, like a tearing sheet. A thin shaft of light shot through the darkness from above and landed on his head. The shadows pulled back, or maybe the beam got wider, or both. Whatever was happening, he was drenched in light.

"Chad!" This time he saw me. "Let's get out of here!"

He scrambled to his feet and stumbled toward us. The nun turned. More light came down. In front of us. Blinding. And the nun was gone. Vanished. But the light remained, forming a path. I grabbed Chad's hand and we ran as fast as we could.

His scenes began playing in the crystals around us. More than once I had to pull him away—after all they were about him. But we followed the path 'til there were no more, 'til we reached the edge of the snowflake and its frosty wall.

"Now what?" he said.

I had no idea. But since I could see the path kept on going beyond the snowflake, I figured why not. I closed my eyes, walked forward and stepped through the wall. Chad followed.

But instead of being with the other snowflakes or even looking down on Earth, we were outside the Gate's wall, freezing our butts off.

"Miss Brenda?" Cowboy's voice. I could barely hear him through the wind. "Miss Brenda, you there?"

"Yeah," I shouted. "We're here."

"Thank the Lord," he said. "You gotta hurry back. We just lost Chad. Don't need to lose you, too."

"No such luck," I shouted. "He's here with me

now."

"That's not possible."

"Guess you'll have to tell him that." I turned to Chad, but he wasn't moving. His eyes stared lifelessly.

"Hey!" I waved my hand in front of him. Nothing. "Hey!"

"He ain't there, Miss Brenda."

"No." I reached over and shook him. "He's right here." But he didn't move. He didn't breathe. I shook him harder.

"He's gone. Now you gotta get back—"

"No." I grabbed him by the collar. "He's with me."

"Miss Bren—"

Bein' stubborn has its plusses and minuses. I didn't know which this would be. But I did know one thing.

I pulled him forward. "He's with me and we're comin' back!"

Chapter 15

It wasn't hard willing me and Chad back into the portal. But staying in the center of it was tougher than I thought. Still, we'd come this far, no way was I giving up now. "Keep doing that CPR," I shouted. "Don't let up."

"It's no use." This time it was Andi. "He's gone."

"No! I'm bringing him home!"

Course it might of been easier if the guy wasn't dead weight. It took both hands just to hang on to him, which kept throwing us off balance and causing us to bang along the tunnel's wall like a pinball.

No problem—'cept for those snarling, frog-faced things. Seems every time we slammed into one, we picked it up as a hitchhiker. Creepy? Yeah. But not as creepy as them crawling over us. I tried not to panic, but Stephie and them must of saw it on my sensors.

"You okay?" Cowboy asked.

"Yeah," I said. "It's just these things."

"What things?"

I watched one climbing up Chad's chest toward his face.

"Go on!" I shouted. "Leave him alone!"

"What things?"

"These gremlin things. The ones I sketched, they—" I gasped as it crawled up his neck and onto his face.

"Demons, Miss Brenda? You talkin' 'bout them demons you drew?"

"I don't know what I'm talking about, but—"

I watched as it pried open Chad's lips with its talons then suddenly dissolved. Not dissolved, really. More like turned misty. A mist that shot into his mouth and down his throat.

I might of screamed a little.

"Miss Brenda?"

Another was scampering right behind it. It leaped on his face where it also dissolved and shot down his throat. Then another behind it. Like they were playing follow the leader.

I felt something on my own stomach. I looked down and saw one crawlin' up me, too. "Wake me up," I shouted. "Get me outta here!"

"We can't." Stephie said. You could hear the emotion in her voice. "You've got to do it yourself or it could damage your limbic system."

I watched the first one move up my chest. It was slimy, wart-covered and had a nasty overbite.

"I don't care what it damages. I don't want these

things in me!"

There was no answer.

"Hello? Anybody?"

Cowboy came back on. "Miss Brenda? Will you pray with me?"

"What!?"

"We got the power. We got the authority."

"Cowboy!"

"All we got to do is use it."

The thing had reached the base of my neck. I heard its fangs gnashing and clicking. I clenched my jaw shut. Shouted through gritted teeth: "Anything! Just do it!"

"All right, then," he said. "Demons of hell—"

It crawled up my neck.

"—I command you by the authority of Jesus Christ—"

Now it was on my chin—claws poking and prodding, looking for an opening.

"—leave!" Cowboy shouted. "Go!"

Nothing happened.

"Miss Brenda, you got to agree with me. Brenda?"

I swallowed and gave a hm-mm, which was about all I could come up with. And it was about all I needed. 'Cause when Cowboy shouted, "Go!" again, something happened. Something brushed against my face. Wind, but harder. At the same time I heard a smack and saw the thing flying off, squealing as it fell into the tunnel.

The others that had been following it up my chest froze. But Cowboy wasn't done.

"Do you hear me?" he shouted. "In the name of Jesus Christ, I order you to leave!"

Their heads swiveled, eyes filled with panic.

"All of you! Leave! Now!"

I felt another blast of wind. Heard the things shrieking and screaming as they got swept off, tumbling into the darkness.

But they didn't leave Chad. When I turned to him I saw a line of 'em continuing to run up his chest and leap into his mouth.

"Cowboy," I shouted. "What about Chad? You've got to—"

Stephie interrupted. "You're at level now. Take a breath. Force yourself to wake."

"But—"

"Now! Hurry!"

I did like she said. I took a breath and made my eyes open. The light was bright, but there was Andi and Cowboy staring down at me. It took some doing, but I turned my head toward Chad in the other chair. He was anything but dead. His body twisted and fought against the restraints, his eyes bulging.

"I thought—" my throat was dry as sand. "I thought he was dead."

Cowboy explained as Andi removed the sensors. "We did like you said. We kept up the CPR. But then . . ." He didn't finish.

Stephie stood beside Chad, stroking his head, trying to calm him, but he would have none of it. "We read about this in the Army logs," she said. "We knew it was a risk, but we never—"

"Read about what?" I asked.

"Sometimes the subjects—" she tried to be calm and brave, but that's hard when someone is snapping and snarling at you like a wild animal. "Sometimes they returned with severe mental illness." She looked down at him. "Schizophrenia. Or worse."

"That ain't schizophrenia," Cowboy said. "That's demons."

"Demons?" Andi repeated.

"That's what was attacking Miss Brenda."

They looked to me and I answered. "It was something."

"But she's okay," Stephie said. "How come she's okay and Chad, he's—"

"Cause I took authority," Cowboy said. "Miss Brenda agreed and I used my authority to—"

"Then I'll do it," she said, "with Chad."

"I don't think that's such a—"

She turned to the kid and shouted, "Demons!"

"Miss Stephie, I don't—"

"I command you to leave Chad."

No response. Just more snarling and snapping.

"Like I said—" Cowboy came to a stop as Chad's eyes flew open.

"Chad!" Stephie cried. "You're back." She threw her arms around him.

He opened his mouth, tried to say something.

"What?" she said. She lowered her ear to his lips.

He tried again, a low, raspy whisper.

"Yes!" she said. "Until you're stronger, of course I'll take them. Then we can both find a way to—"

"Miss Steph—!"

But Cowboy was too late. She gave a startled cry. Her head flew back. Her eyes widened and she began choking.

"Stephie?" Andi shouted.

"No," Chad wheezed, trying to talk. "That wasn't me."

"Miss Stephie, are you—"

"A trick." Chad coughed. "They tricked her—"

Stephie cut him off with a scream—more like a howl, deep and from her gut. Then she doubled over, gagging, holding herself up by the medical cart between me and Chad.

"It's them," Cowboy shouted. "They've left him and gone into her."

"Do something!" I yelled. "Cowboy, do—"

"In the name of Jesus." He stepped toward her. "In the name of Jesus Christ, I—"

She came up fast, medical tray in hand. She slammed it hard into his face. Harder than a person her size could swing. Cowboy staggered backward. Andi tried to catch him, but was no match for his weight. They fell to the ground, Cowboy thumping his head on the tile floor. Not bad, but enough to leave him dazed.

"Tank!" Andi shouted to him. "Are you all right?"

Meanwhile Stephie bolted out the door. Out the door and out the building.

"Stop her!" Chad shouted. "Before they—" He broke into a coughing fit. Tried to move, but the sensors and restraints held him down.

I threw my feet over the side of my recliner and rose. Things went white a moment and I had to reach out and steady myself. Andi stayed on the floor helping Cowboy as Chad kept yelling, "Stop her! Somebody!"

I finally got my head clear enough to stumble out of the room. My sprained ankle didn't help. "Stephie!"

Outside, the late afternoon sun blinded me, but I caught movement near the highway and limped after her. "Stephie!"

She heard my voice as she reached the highway

and stopped and turned.

"Come back in," I yelled. "Let Cowboy help. We all can—"

Her voice was deep and guttural. "You have no idea what you're dealing with."

The tone gave me chills and I slowed to a stop.

"You think you can stop us?" she said.

I cleared my throat. "Stop who?"

"Have you not read your own scriptures?" Before I could answer, her face twisted with pain. "Help me." It was Stephie's voice. "Please. Help—" She stooped over, like she was fighting something, then rose with the other voice. "Continue down this path and your fate will be no different than your partner's."

"My part—Are you talking about the professor?"

An approaching eighteen-wheeler hit its horn—the driver obviously not thrilled with someone standing so close to his lane. Stephie turned to it, then back to me. An ugly smile filled her face. More like a leer.

My mind raced, fearing the worse. I started toward her. "No, Stephie. Don't. Whatever you're thinking—"

She turned back to the truck. It was coming fast, horn blasting.

"No!"

She sprinted toward it.

"Steph—"

She darted into its lane. The driver hit the brakes, wheels screeching, smoke rolling off its tires.

If she screamed, I didn't hear. The semi hit her. Dead center. It threw her into the air. She hit the pavement, bouncing like a doll—until the left front tire caught up and rolled over her.

Chad's scream drifted out of the building. "Stephie!" He hadn't seen what happened, but somehow he knew. And even where I stood, you could hear his agony. "Stephie . . ."

Epilogue

"You sure you ladies are gonna be okay?" Cowboy asked as he tossed Andi's backpack into the rear seat of my car.

"No worries," I said. "Stephie got the hose patched up good enough to get us to town. We'll get it repaired there."

"Or scrap it," Cowboy joked.

"Not this baby." I opened the door and climbed in. "It's a collector's piece. Can't buy nothing like this at a car dealership."

"She's got a point," Andi said, fighting to open the

passenger's door. Cowboy joined in and after two or three tugs it cooperated with a sickening groan.

"We'll have them look at that, too," I said.

Andi climbed in, looked back at the lab. "It kills me to know you're going to completely destroy the place."

Chad leaned down to her open window. "Not destroy it. Dismantle it. I'll probably get fifteen, maybe twenty grand for all the stuff."

"But the research, the possibilities. I mean, it brought us to the Gate."

"We don't need the occult to get there," Cowboy said, "not if we're workin' for the good guys."

"You keep using that word, *occult*," I said. "What's the difference between that and what we're doin'?'"

"We're using our God-given gifts. The occult is when you try to barge into the supernatural on your own."

Chad agreed. "And with gifts like mine, who needs to barge?"

Andi turned away from him, rolling her eyes. It had been seventy-two hours since we lost Stephie. Chad had been mostly silent and sullen. When we offered to stay and help with the cremation and all, he said it wasn't necessary. But we all noticed he didn't put up much of a fight when we insisted. And later, when we helped pack her stuff to send to her folks, I saw him slip her white stocking cap into his coat pocket. I didn't say nothing. I knew he knew.

But all good things come to an end, and slowly, his pain-in-the-butt ego was resurfacing.

"Sorry we never found your professor friend," he said. I nodded. But he wasn't done. "'Course if I was on my own, it would have been a different matter.

But having to hang back and show you the ropes definitely cramped my style."

Andi and I traded looks, wondering what reality the kid was visiting now.

"Yeah," I said. "Sorry for being such a bother."

"It happens," he said. "No worries."

Seriously? He'd not caught my sarcasm?

"What about our bosses," Andi asked him. "The Watchers? Any message you want us to deliver to them?"

"Tell them I may reconsider. If their offer is good enough, I may be willing to talk."

"Offer?" Cowboy said. "As in pay?"

"Naturally. A person would be crazy to do this stuff for free."

We all got silent. Andi might have coughed a little.

He just looked at us. "You're kidding me, right?"

We didn't say a word—which we were finding wasn't so necessary around him.

He shook his head. "Amazing. You guys are amazing"

I fired up the car. "Saving the world?" I called out to him. "That ain't enough for you?"

"Not even close."

I shook my own head and ground the gears 'til I found first.

"Drive safe," Cowboy said. "And give Daniel a howdy for me."

"Will do," I called.

"You boys behave yourselves," Andi said.

"Don't worry about us, sweet cheeks," Chad said. We'll have this place cleared in a week—with plenty of time to take this good ol' boy of yours into town and show him a thing or two."

"I wouldn't be taking any bets on that," I shouted through the window as I pulled up to the highway.

"That's right," Andi called back to them. "He and the good Lord may have a thing or two to show *you*."

"Amen!" I shouted.

We laughed and waved goodbye as we turned onto the highway. It was supposed to be a joke. But when I glanced into the rearview mirror, I saw Cowboy nodding thoughtfully and slapping his big hand on Chad's shoulder.

I had to smile. Chad Thorton had no idea what was in store for him.

Then again, I guess none of us did.

Don't miss the other books in the Harbingers series which can be purchased separately or in collections:

CYCLE ONE: INVITATION
The Call
The House
The Sentinels
The Girl

CYCLE TWO: MOSAIC
The Revealing
Infestation
Infiltration

The Fog

CYCLE THREE: The Probing
Leviathan
The Mind Pirates
Hybrids
The Village

OTHER BOOKS BY BILL MYERS

NOVELS
Child's Play
The Judas Gospel
The God Hater
The Voice
Angel of Wrath
The Wager
Soul Tracker
The Presence
The Seeing
The Face of God
When the Last Leaf Falls
Eli
Blood of Heaven
Threshold
Fire of Heaven

NON-FICTION
The Jesus Experience—Journey Deeper into the Heart of God
Supernatural Love
Supernatural War

CHILDREN BOOKS
Baseball for Breakfast (picture book)
The Bug Parables (picture book series)
Bloodstone Chronicles (fantasy series)
McGee and Me (book/video series)
The Incredible Worlds of Wally McDoogle (comedy series)
Bloodhounds, Inc. (mystery series)
The Elijah Project (supernatural suspense series)

Secret Agent Dingledorf and His Trusty Dog Splat (comedy series)

TJ and the Time Stumblers (comedy series)

Truth Seekers (action adventure series)

TEEN BOOKS

Forbidden Doors (supernatural suspense)
  Dark Power Collection
  Invisible Terror Collection
  Deadly Loyalty Collection
  Ancient Forces Collection

For a complete list of Bill's books, sample chapters, and newsletter signup go to *www.Billmyers.com* Or check out his Facebook page: *www.facebook.com/billmyersauthor.*

Made in the USA
Middletown, DE
29 May 2016